for Madelon

Library of Congress Cataloging in Publication Data
Galdone, Paul.   King of the Cats.   "A Clarion book."
Summary: As the gravedigger tells his wife how a band of cats marched into the
cemetery to mourn their dead king, their own cat, Old Tom, listens with a strange
intensity.
  [1. Fairy tales. 2. Folklore—England. 3. Cats—Fiction.] I. Jacobs, Joseph,
1854-1916. The King o' the Cats. II. Title.
PZ8.G127Ki   398.2'452'974428 [E]   79-16659   ISBN 0-395-29030-9
PA ISBN 0-89919-400-1 Rnf H Pap BD 10 9 8 7 6 5 4 3

King of the Cats

A Ghost Story by Joseph Jacobs

Retold and Illustrated by PAUL GALDONE

CLARION BOOKS
TICKNOR & FIELDS : A HOUGHTON MIFFLIN COMPANY
NEW YORK

One October evening the gravedigger's wife was sitting
by the fireside with her big black cat, Old Tom.
They were waiting for the gravedigger to come home.

They waited and they waited,
but still he didn't come.

At last he came rushing in,
and as he came he called,

"Who's Tom Tildrum?"

He said it in such a wild way that
both his wife and his cat
stared at him in fright.

"Why, what's the matter?" said his wife.
"And why do you want to know who Tom Tildrum is?"

"Oh, I've had such an adventure," said the gravedigger.

"I was digging away at old Mr. Fordyce's grave when I suppose I must have dropped asleep.

I only woke up when I heard a cat's

Miaow."

"Miaow,"

said Old Tom in answer.

"Yes, just like that!"
said the gravedigger.

"So I looked over the edge of the grave,
  and what do you think I saw?"
"Now, how can I tell?" said his wife.
"Why, nine black cats, all like our friend Tom here."

"All of them had white spots on their chests,
and what do you think they were carrying?
Why, a small coffin covered with a velvet pall.
On the pall was a small coronet of gold, and
at every third step they took they cried all together,

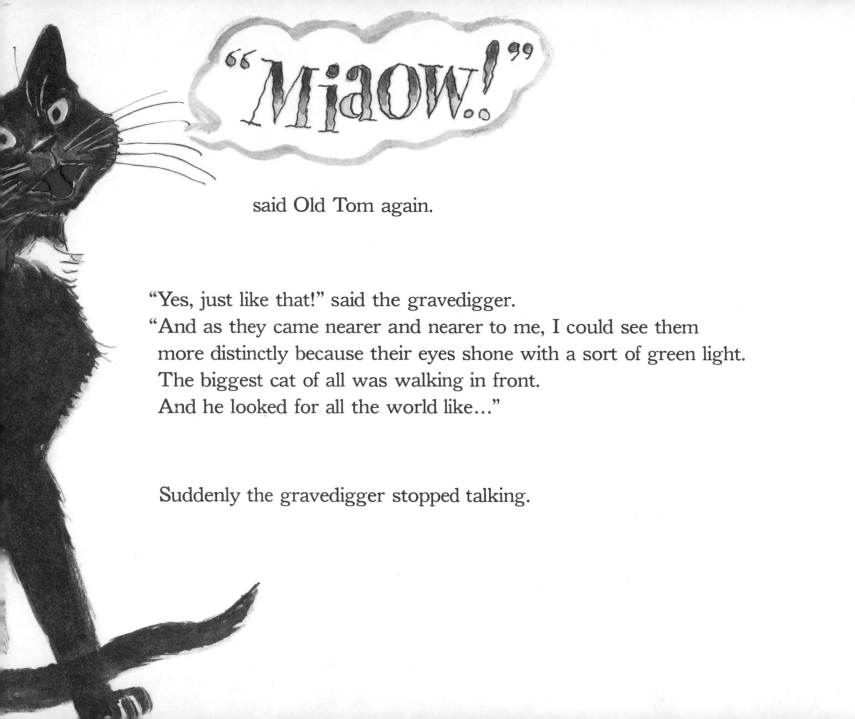

"Miaow!"

said Old Tom again.

"Yes, just like that!" said the gravedigger.
"And as they came nearer and nearer to me, I could see them
more distinctly because their eyes shone with a sort of green light.
The biggest cat of all was walking in front.
And he looked for all the world like..."

Suddenly the gravedigger stopped talking.

"Just look at our Tom, how he's looking at me,"
 the gravedigger said.
"You'd think he knew all I was saying."

"Go on, go on," said his wife.
"Never mind Old Tom."

"Well, as I was a-saying,
the nine cats came toward
me slowly and solemnly.
And at every third step
they all cried together—"

"**Miaow!**"
said Old Tom again.

"Yes, just like that,"
said the gravedigger.

"The cats came on and on till they stood right opposite
Mr. Fordyce's grave, where I was.

Then they all stood still and looked straight at me.
I did feel queer, that I did!"

"But look at Old Tom," said the gravedigger. "He's looking at me just like they did."

"Go on, go on," said his wife.
"Never mind Old Tom."

"Where was I?" said the gravedigger.
"Oh, yes. There they all stood, still
looking at me, when the one that wasn't
carrying the coffin came forward.
Staring straight at me, he
said to me—yes, I tell you, he
said to me, in a squeaky voice,

And that's why I asked
you if you knew
who Tom Tildrum was,
for how can I tell
Tom Tildrum that
Tim Toldrum's dead
if I don't know who
Tom Tildrum is?"

"Look at Old Tom, look at Old Tom!" screamed
the gravedigger's wife. And well he might look,
for Tom was swelling and Tom was staring
and at last Tom shrieked out,

"What—old Tim dead!
Then I, Tom Tildrum, am
King of the Cats!"

And Old Tom rushed up the chimney
and was never seen again.